Ashley's Yellow Ribbon

Barbara Davoll

Illustrations by
Joe VanSeveren

MOODY PRESS
CHICAGO

Dedicated to the brave men and women
of Operation Desert Storm
who have made us all proud Americans.

With many thanks to Andy deLivron and his wife Nancy
for their support, encouragement, and help with this project.
And particularly to their daughters, Kathy and Becky,
for their critique from Ashley's point of view.

© 1991 by
THE MOODY BIBLE INSTITUTE
OF CHICAGO

ISBN: 0-8024-0815-X

1 2 3 4 5 6 Printing/DP/Year 95 94 93 92 91

Printed in the United States of America

Ashley leaned her bike against the porch, grabbed her bookbag, and bounded through the front door, letting it slam.

"Hey, Mom! I'm home!" she yelled, stuffing a warm chocolate chip cookie into her mouth from a plate on the kitchen counter.

''Hi, honey,'' responded her mother, coming into the kitchen. ''I see you've found the cookies.''

''Ummm! They're great! Still warm! May I have another?'' asked Ashley hopefully, reaching for a large one bulging with nuts and chocolate.

''Just one more.'' Mother smiled. ''They're for Chad's party tonight. How was school today?''

''OK. I was anxious to get home though, to help you get ready for the party.''

Ashley felt sad inside to think that her fun-loving brother was entering the army helicopter program and would no longer be at home to give her a ride on his motorcycle and tease her. Sometimes he was a pain, but he was never too busy to rescue Cougar, her gray kitten, from the tree in the backyard or to fix her bike when the chain came off.

Since that evening was Chad's last night at home, supper was special. Mom had outdone herself with all of Chad's favorites. Ashley pushed her peas around on her plate. *Yuk!* Peas surely weren't *her* favorite, but she guessed she could eat them since they were fixed especially for Chad.

"I heard on the news today that things aren't going well over in the Middle East," commented her father. "The President says there will be war if they continue as they are."

Ashley felt a little knot in her stomach. That word *war* was scary to her. Especially since Chad was joining the army. If a war came, maybe he would be in it.

"Daddy," she asked fearfully, "will Chad be in the war? Because if he is, I don't want him to go." And Ashley began to cry.

"Hey, Squirt! You're getting tears in your mashed potatoes, and the whole mess is going to run right off your plate," teased Chad. "I'm just going into training. I'll only be a few hours away for now, so I can come home often. You and Mom and Dad can come down to camp and see me too. Won't that be fun?" he asked, leaning over and wiping her tears with his napkin.

"I guess so, but I'd like it a lot better if you'd stay here," Ashley gulped, trying not to cry.

After the party that night Ashley lay in bed thinking. *Will there still be good times after Chad is gone?* she wondered. *Why do things always have to change?*

One winter afternoon after Chad left, when
Ashley came home from school her mother was
watching television. ''The President is speaking,''
said Mother. ''He has just announced that we are at
war,'' she added sadly.

Ashley felt the knot in her tummy again. *Chad
will go to war,* she thought. Her plans to play with her
friends after school didn't seem important now.
Nothing else seemed to matter.

When it was time for Ashley to go to bed, both of
her parents went upstairs with her. As she climbed
into bed her father sat down on the edge of the bed
and said gently, "Honey, I know you are worried
about the war and about Chad. We had a call from
him today telling us that he will be leaving this week
for the war zone."

Ashley began to cry. ''Why, Daddy? Why does he have to go? Not everyone has to go. Why does Chad?''

''Because Chad has volunteered, honey. That means that he offered to go. No one made him. He loves his country and wants to do his part.''

''But, Daddy, will there be fighting—and killing—and bombs?'' Ashley's eyes were round with fear. She had seen a television program one time when someone had thrown a bomb and a whole building blew up. Now Chad would be where there were bombs and guns.

"Yes, Ashley. There will be guns and bombs, and there will be killing too. War is a terrible thing—but there is something worse than that."

Ashley looked at her father wildly as tears ran down her face. *Something worse that that! What did Daddy mean?* "How can—anything—be—worse?"

Mother was kneeling beside her bed stroking her hair.

"Ashley, I think it would be far worse if men who make war and do bad things are allowed to continue to do those bad things and are never stopped. Wouldn't that be much worse?" asked her father kindly.

Ashley looked at her father, still sobbing, but she was thinking. *Yes, that would be worse. For then the war and killing would go on and on.*

"That is why good men like our Chad must go," continued her father. "So that men who do terrible, wicked things will be stopped."

"Oh, but Daddy, I'm so afraid. Maybe Chad will be hurt or die."

"Ashley, dear, listen to me. Our God is
protecting Chad just as He is protecting you and me
and Mother. Did you know that Chad will be just as
safe in the war as we are here?"

Ashley shook her head. *How can Chad be just as
safe as we are? There aren't any bombs here.*

"Honey, the Bible tells us it doesn't matter
where we are—how dangerous the situation—God is
our protection. Let me show you a verse in the Bible
that tells us that."

Then her father picked up Ashley's Bible from her nightstand. In his calm soothing voice he read a beautiful verse that made the knot of fear in her stomach feel much better. He read Proverbs 21:31:

The horse is prepared for battle,
but safety is of the Lord.

"This verse tells us that no matter where we are—at home where we aren't in great danger—or even in war—our safety depends upon the Lord."

"Does that mean we won't die?" asked Ashley.

"No, it doesn't mean that," answered her father.
"The Bible tells us that all men will die sometime.
That time is decided by God alone. Because Chad is
a child of God he is totally in the hands of his loving
heavenly Father, who is caring for him and knows
what is best. We have to trust the Lord for Chad's
safety and for everything in our own lives too."
Father held Ashley's hand in his large one.

After prayer Ashley lay quietly while Mother continued to stroke her hair. Soon she was sound asleep, and her parents tiptoed out of the room, turning off the light.

The next few days, although Ashley felt better about Chad's being called to war, there were things that still made her fearful. One thing that made her feel afraid was all the war news on television.

Another thing that troubled her was a fear that maybe the war would someday reach her city. Sometimes at night she lay listening, imagining she heard airplanes coming to drop bombs on her.

One evening a very loud plane flew low above
her house, and Ashley jumped up scattering her
paper dolls everywhere. ''Oh Daddy, are they
coming?'' she cried.

When her father realized how afraid she was, he took her in his arms and held her tightly. He told her that the war was thousands of miles away, and Ashley was not quite so afraid after that.

One afternoon when she went shopping with her father she saw a crowd. They were all carrying signs, and they looked very unhappy. The people were surrounded by policemen.

"Who are they, Daddy?" she asked pointing at the group.

"Those are war protesters, Ashley. They are people who don't feel we should be fighting the war," her father answered. "Most of them feel there is never a good reason for war."

Ashley didn't think too highly of the protesters who disagreed with her father and brother. She wanted to go right over and tell them a thing or two. "I don't think they should do that," she said indignantly.

"That is the wonderful thing about our country, Ashley. We are free to say what we think, without others stopping us," answered her father.

That night on television a news reporter told about some families of soldiers who had tied yellow ribbons around their trees to show that they loved and supported the soldiers. Ashley thought that was a lovely idea. She wondered why no one had thought to do that in her town. Suddenly she had an idea—but she wouldn't tell anyone about it just yet. She had to do some planning first.

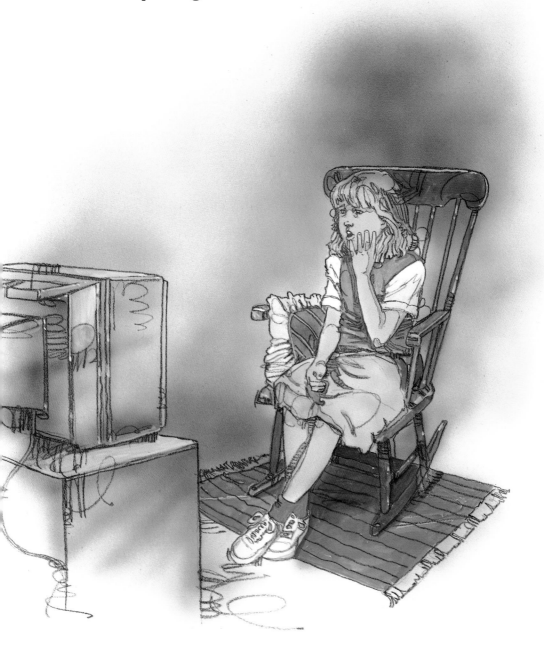

The next day after school Ashley started down the street pulling her red wagon behind her. Her first stop was at the Jordan house next door. Walking up to the door she swallowed nervously and rang the bell. When her neighbor came to the door Ashley said, "Hello, Mrs. Jordan. Do you have any soda cans I could recycle for you? I'm collecting them to raise money for a project to help our soldiers."

Mrs. Jordan smiled down at her. "Why, of course I do. I've a whole box waiting to be taken back. I'll get them for you."

Every afternoon Ashley visited home after home in her neighborhood, collecting all the soda cans she could. As soon as her wagon was full she would pull it to the neighborhood recycling center and collect money for the cans.

When Saturday came she proudly counted her money. She had enough to buy one roll of yellow ribbon. Deciding it was time to let her parents know about her project, she showed them her money and asked them to take her to the store.

As they drove downtown Ashley wriggled around in her seat belt with excitement. Her eyes were shining as she laid her money on the counter at the store. ''May I have this roll of yellow ribbon, please?'' she asked. ''It's for our soldiers,'' she explained. As the clerk handed her the ribbon Ashley said cheerfully, ''You'd better order more of this. I'm going to need lots more.''

Then Father said, "Let's get three more rolls right now, and I'll pay for it."

Ashley gave him a happy hug.

From that day on Ashley didn't notice the little knot in her tummy. She was happily making yellow bows from the ribbon she bought. No one in town had a yellow ribbon yet, but Ashley meant to change all of that. With the help of her parents she was able to make a lot of bows in a short time. Ashley was so excited she could hardly stand it! She was planning a wonderful surprise!

One evening when most of the town was asleep, Ashley and her parents began to decorate their porch and front yard—putting the ribbons on the trees, the porch banisters, the front door—wherever they could. By the time they were finished, the outside of their home was beautifully decorated with a new flag and yellow bows. Then Ashley's father helped her make a sign.

SUPPORT
OUR
TROOPS
FREE YELLOW
RIBBONS HERE!

The next day the whole school was talking about the yellow ribbons in Ashley's yard. That evening there was a traffic jam in front of Ashley's house. The reason for all of the traffic was the sign Ashley had made. It was leaning against a tree in the yard, and Ashley was standing beside it giving away yellow bows to all who stopped. Before the week was over nearly every house and store in their little town was waving an American flag and wearing a yellow ribbon.

Ashley drew a picture of the town with all its flags and ribbons and asked her mother to send it to Chad. Then she had another idea. Maybe some of her friends at school could write to Chad and the other soldiers.

Her mother got a list of all the servicemen from their area, and Ashley took it to school. The principal thought she had a good idea, and they started a writing project for all the students. Soon the post office was bulging with sacks of mail written to the soldiers. It seemed that nearly everyone in town was writing to them.

Ashley wrote to many of the soldiers also, but
the highlight for her was when she heard from Chad.
She loved his funny letters all about the army.

But suddenly the letters from Chad stopped coming. Day after day went by, and there was no word from him. Ashley could tell that her parents were worried. Although she had been praying every day for Chad, she began to pray more. The little knot of fear came back to her tummy. *Why was Chad not writing? Could he be injured or even dead? Maybe he was being held prisoner.* Those terrible thoughts were never far from her mind, and sometimes the yellow ribbons seemed to mock her. *Chad will never see us,* they seemed to say.

Although worried, Ashley continued to write to the other soldiers and pray for them and Chad. Somehow their letters made her feel closer to her brother. As the days dragged into weeks she could hardly think of anything but Chad and his safety.

Cougar, a good-sized cat by now, became Ashley's constant companion. He was always ready to snuggle up to her for a cozy time and seemed to understand just how she felt. When Ashley felt sad she would hold Cougar close and pray for Chad. Cougar would purr his sympathy and lick her with his rough tongue. Then Ashley would feel better.

One spring morning Ashley was sitting on the porch steps cuddling Cougar. A tear slipped its way down her cheek as she thought of Chad and wondered if they would ever hear from him again. Suddenly she heard the phone ring. Her mother answered as usual, and then Ashley heard her gasp. "Chad! Oh, Chad, is it really you?!"

Ashley dumped the surprised Cougar, who had been enjoying his warm morning nap on her lap, and raced into the kitchen. Her mother stood holding the phone, looking as if she might faint.

"Mom? What is it? Is it Chad?" Ashley could hardly get her breath. Was it really her brother?

Her mother motioned for her to be quiet as she was straining to hear. "Chad, dear, are you all right? We've been so worried," she said brokenly with tears. After some more conversation, Mother handed the phone to Ashley, who was also crying by now.

"Hello! Chad, this is Ashley. Where are you?"

From very far away came the sound of Chad's voice. He sounded weak, but it was definitely Chad. He had been injured behind enemy lines, and some kind people in the countryside had kept him alive until it was safe for the army medics to go in and get him. His right arm was severely injured. But he was recovering now in an army hospital, and they would be sending him home soon.

When they hung up the phone Ashley and her mother cried and hugged each other and then thanked God for keeping Chad safe. Ashley felt sad that Chad had been so terribly injured, but he was alive! With great excitement they called Father, who took the rest of the day off to be with them and to help call their friends and relatives with the glad news. What a time of rejoicing for them—their Chad was coming home!

Then there was more excitement! Chad was coming home a hero! He had saved several of his buddies from death with his brave actions. The town would have a special homecoming ceremony for him. And he had been awarded a Purple Heart medal.

The morning of Chad's homecoming was a clear, blue-sky day. As Ashley rode to the airport with her parents the town had never looked lovelier. All of the flags and yellow ribbons moved gently in the breeze as if to say, "Chad's coming! Chad's coming!"

And then he was there, walking with a cane, his injured arm hanging useless in its sleeve. He was much thinner but looking extremely handsome in his uniform. And there was that special one-arm hug just for her—his Squirt. Oh, life was too wonderful at that moment. "God, You are so good," whispered Ashley on the way back to the ceremony.

"What's with all these yellow bows, Squirt?" asked Chad as they drove through town. "Are these the ones you made? They sure are beautiful," he said happily, giving her a squeeze.

Ashley nodded with pride. A lump in her throat wouldn't allow her to answer out loud. Chad was seeing them after all.

And then the ceremony began. Ashley sat on the platform with her parents as the band played the ''Star Spangled Banner.'' Some of her yellow ribbons decorated the platform. It seemed to Ashley that the whole world was red, white, and blue—and yellow. Now the mayor was giving a speech telling how Chad's bravery had saved lives.

After he finished, Chad came to the microphone to say a few words. He wore his beautiful medal, shaped like a heart, on his uniform.

''Friends and loved ones,'' he began, ''it is so good to be home and to have these kind words said about me. What I did was simply what a soldier should do. The real heroes are the ones who will not come home from this war. They are the ones who have died for a cause greater than themselves. I am deeply thankful to God for bringing me home safely. I am also grateful for the peace He gave me when I was facing death that, if I were killed, I would have a home in heaven waiting for me. Thank you for all of your love and prayers.''

As Chad sat down the townspeople roared their approval with applause and cheers. Ashley sat swinging her legs and watching as if she were in a dream. Then something happened that quickly brought her back to reality.

The people were cheering, and now the mayor
was standing in front of Ashley. Her parents stood
and pulled her up with them. She heard her name!
What was it the mayor had said? That he knew of her
efforts with the yellow ribbons and how she had
prayed for her brother and the troops—and how all
the letters and pictures from the children had cheered
the soldiers at the front. Now the mayor was bending
low and hanging a wide yellow ribbon around Ashley's
neck, from which hung a large shiny medal.

"This medal is given to you by your town, my dear, for the difference you've made here and in many lives." Ashley's father then lifted her into Chad's good arm and stood with him, helping him hold her. The people cheered again, and Ashley's yellow ribbon, with its medal, caught the sunlight.

"Don't you get too proud, Squirt," whispered her big brother, teasing, "or I'll take you down a notch or two. I've still got one good arm, you know."

Ashley looked at him out of the corner of her eye. Her wonderful brother was home—but she could tell that he would still be a pain sometimes. "I'll hit you with my medal," she warned. "It's bigger than yours," she added under her breath as they waved and smiled.

Although this war was coming to a close and things were coming back to normal for Ashley, some things would never be the same again. There was Chad's terrible injury, and other brothers would still face the dangers of war in different places around the world. She had grown up a lot while Chad had been away. She was learning that although life was not always easy, God could be trusted to do what is best for His children.

She looked down at her new yellow ribbon with the medal winking at her in the sun. It would always remind her of God's answer to her prayers for Chad and that she could make a difference.

Discussion Helps for Parents and Teachers

The moving story of Ashley and her family may serve as a springboard to discuss some of the fears your children have about war, death, and separation from loved ones. As with all childhood concerns, there are no magic answers for these questions. Discussing them with a loving caregiver, however, can be beneficial and lead to lines of communication being open for other situations that may arise.

As the children express their feelings it is important to convey to them that God loves them and is in control of all things, even when they are in danger. Two Scripture verses are comforting: ''What time I am afraid, I will trust in thee'' (Psalm 56:3), and, ''In God have I put my trust: I will not be afraid of what man can do unto me'' (Psalm 56:11).

This would be a good opportunity to stress the need for a personal salvation experience so that the children may have the assurance of a home in heaven and the joy of trusting Christ (John 3:16 and 14:1-3).

It is also important to convey to the children that no matter what traumas occur in their lives, they will be lovingly cared for by the guardians who are responsible for them. Sometimes just a hug and the statement ''I am here and I will always take good care of you'' is enough. Knowing you will love and care for them will go a long way in providing the warmth and emotional security they need to face our uncertain world.